# Zack Black and the Magic Dads

## by
## Annie Dalton

### Illustrated by Ross Collins

You do not need to read this page –
just get on with the book!

First published in 2007 in Great Britain by
Barrington Stoke Ltd
18 Walker Street, Edinburgh, EH3 7LP

www.barringtonstoke.co.uk

Reprinted 2008

ISBN: 978-1-84299-384-2

Printed in Great Britain by Bell & Bain Ltd

## AUTHOR ID

**Name:** Annie Dalton

**Likes:** Singing when I'm by myself in my car.

**Dislikes:** Dead mice under my bed. My cats leave them as presents.

**3 words that best describe me:**
Tall, shy, dreamer.

**A secret not many people know:**
I'm addicted to Bollywood movies!

## ILLUSTRATOR ID

**Name:** Ross Collins

**Likes:** Running without scissors.

**Dislikes:** Running with scissors.

**3 words that best describe me:**
I'm Ross Collins.

**A secret not many people know:**
I'm not Ross Collins.

To Mark, who already has a cool dad

# Contents

# Chapter 1

# The Perfect Dad

I didn't want a new dad, that's the mad part. I was totally OK with being in a one parent family. I went to the Magic Dads website because of my mum!

I wasn't one of those sad one-parent kids you read about in books. I never felt I was missing out. I had a grandma and a grandpa who loved me to bits. I had a cool aunt, loads of mates. Why did I need a dad? I didn't think I did!

Here are four true things I know about my real dad:

**1.** His name was Mike Black.

**2.** He always picked the tomato out of his cheese and tomato sandwiches.

**3.** He liked to turn his music up loud when he was driving.

**4.** He loved us at first, then when I was one year old he stopped.

It sounds sad when you say it like that. I bet I was really sad at the time. But if you asked me if I miss him now, I'd say, 'nah!'

My mum's a star. After my dad left she went to do an art course at our local college. She turned out to be a really good artist. People are always ringing her up because they want to buy her stuff.

She can do anything she wants to, my mum. She can put up shelves, fix her own car. And every Saturday she comes to watch me play football. Rain or shine she's there shouting for my team.

I was happy living with Mum. Plus – I don't mean to be big-headed – but Mum seemed totally happy living with me!

Then one morning she was checking her e-mails and up popped a message from her best friend Nat. Nat had just got married to an American guy. She met him on the internet. Now Nat and her little boy were in America with her new husband. Mum misses them a lot.

I was going to be late for school so I left Mum reading Nat's email and catching up on her friend's news.

As I walked out of our front door everything seemed normal. No thunder or flashes of lightning. Nothing at all to tell me this was my last day as a happy one-parent kid.

I did see an old camper van parked across the road from my house. It was green and rusty and it had curtains. They were closed. It was raining. I noticed that too.

It was still raining when I walked back from school. The minute I walked in my house something felt wrong.

There were pictures everywhere. Pictures of me.

On the TV was a picture of a cute little baby riding on its dad's back. Me again.

Mum had been watching our old home movies. Now she was sitting on the floor crying.

I'd never seen Mum cry before. OK, sometimes she cries when she watches a DVD. But not in real life, with the front door open so anyone could see.

I whispered, "Mum?" My heart was thumping.

Mum sat up in a hurry. "Zack! Is it home time already?" She quickly wiped her eyes. "I was just being silly! I'm fine now."

At tea time she stirred her pasta around and didn't say a word.

At last she took a deep breath. "Are you happy, Zack?" she said. "I want you to tell me the truth."

I was surprised. "I'm totally happy! Why?"

Mum frowned. "You must feel sad sometimes that you don't have a dad."

"I don't, actually," I told her.

"What about on Sports Day when they have the Fathers' Race?" Mum asked.

"Gramps always runs in the Fathers' Race," I pointed out. "He came second this year! He was well chuffed!"

Mum shook her head. "He's your grandpa. A boy needs a proper dad."

Later I heard her talking to my aunt Sarah. "Zack is a wonderful kid. He needs a wonderful dad. Why can't I meet Mr Right like Nat did?"

*So that's what's got Mum so upset*, I thought. She feels like a loser because she can't find a brand new dad to whisk us off to a brand new life, like Nat and her kid.

********

The week-end came and my mum was still really low.

I'm always ace at cheering Mum up. I found some big purple flowers in the garden and stuck them in a jar. I made cups of tea in her favourite blue mug. I told all my best jokes. Nothing worked. She was still sad.

I was worried now. This was bad. I rang my aunt Sarah. "I've tried everything," I told her. "Now it's your turn."

Sarah came round with take-away food.

I sat on the stairs and heard them talking.

I heard Sarah say, "You should try computer dating like Nat."

"I don't want to go on dates," Mum moaned. "I want to find a dad for Zack and live happily ever after."

We were living happily ever after, I thought. We were before Mum got that stupid e-mail.

If you'd lifted the roof off my house that night, you'd have seen me and Mum in different rooms, both wide awake, both wishing, wishing.

You can guess what Mum was wishing. As for me – I was just wishing to get my old chatty happy mum back. Small problem. I couldn't get my wish, until Mum got her wish. Which was never going to happen unless ...

I sat up in the dark.

"Unless I make Mum's wish come true," I whispered.

I had to find the perfect dad. I had to make us all live happily ever after.

I just needed to work out how.

# Chapter 2

# The Great Shaboosh

If you have to shop for a new dad, you really need to know what sort you're looking for!

"How can you tell if someone would be a brilliant dad?" I asked Mum at breakfast.

Mum had been thinking about this a lot!

"A good dad has loads of energy," she said at once. "He's never too tired to hang out with his kids. At week-ends he takes them out on trail bikes, or roller-blading. And he's always in a great mood, laughing and joking."

I quickly wrote down everything Mum said. I had no idea what I was going to do with this info, but it might come in useful.

"Time for school, Zack!" Mum said.

I rushed out of the house. That rusty old van was still parked across the road. Today there was a notice stuck inside one of the windows. It said: **Open – The Great Shaboosh.**

I laughed. "The Great Shaboosh! What sort of a name is that!"

The van's door slid open, making me jump. It was a rainy winter day but the street seemed to fill with super-bright sunshine.

A young guy in dreadlocks looked out. "Are you wanting to see the Great Shaboosh?"

"No, you're all right," I said quickly.

He was still in his teens but something in his eyes made you think twice about laughing at him.

"Are you sure, Zack?" he asked softly. "You look like you could really use some help."

I blinked at him in the strange bright light coming from his van.

He knew my name.

*He knows everything*, I thought. He knows about my mum. He knows I'm shopping for a new dad.

This was too spooky for me. I quickly shook my head.

The door slid shut and the street was dark and rainy again.

My skin was tingling all over. I was 99% sure the Great Shaboosh was some kind of travelling wizard.

At school I couldn't get him out of my mind. Mrs Woods told me off twice for day-dreaming.

At lunch-time my mates wanted me to play football but I had some hard thinking to do. I mooched around the playground with my hands in my pockets.

Could I trust this teenage wizard to make my mum's dream come true? And if the Great Shaboosh was for real, how would I pay him? I only had about 50p!

Suddenly someone walked slap-bang into me. It was Josie Miller with her nose in a book as always. She stomped off rubbing her head. She made a face at me as if it was my fault!

"Try looking where you're going, freak!" I yelled.

When I got back to my house, the Great Shaboosh was just saying good-bye to an old lady.

He smiled when he saw me. "Good man, you came back!"

The old lady was skipping down the street by this time!

"What did she come for?" I asked.

The wizard shook his head. "The Great Shaboosh never talks about his clients."

He sat down and opened up his laptop. He typed with just two fingers but he was really fast.

"That's a cool little machine," I said.

"Thanks! I got it mail order from the 23rd century."

I laughed. "Oh yeah, what can it do?"

"Whatever I want it to do," he said softly.

He was serious! I was looking at a computer from the future!

The Great Shaboosh gave me a big grin. "Sit down, Zack, and tell me what's going on with your mum."

He just wanted to hear me say it. I could tell he knew everything already.

"She thinks she's a rubbish mum because I haven't got a dad. But she won't do computer dating. She wants to just meet someone."

"Won't do computer dating," the Great Shaboosh murmured. "Don't suppose you know what kind of dad she's looking for, Zack?"

"I do! I wrote down everything she said. It's here in my notebook. You can read it if you want," I told him.

"Good man!" The wizard quickly read my notes. "Oh, the Active Dad," he said with a smile. "That's a very popular model."

He typed some words into the computer. Something beeped.

"You're in luck. They've got one in stock!" he grinned.

He made getting a new dad seem like ordering a pizza!

"But – isn't this just like computer dating?" I said.

The wizard looked stern. "Zack, do you want me to help your mum or not?"

"I – but how will I pay you?" I stuttered. A new dad must cost way more than 50p!

"Let's do a swap?" he said. "I send your mum the dad of her dreams. In return, you do a task."

What was he on about? Heroes did tasks. They had to climb a tall mountain or kill dragons. But there weren't any mountains – or any dragons – in my town. But then again, yesterday we didn't have any wizards!

"Deal?" he smiled.

I started to laugh. "Deal!"

The wizard quickly wrote a string of words and numbers in my notebook.

"That's your link for the perfect dad," he said.

He slid open the van door and let out some more of that weird indoor sunshine. I wanted to see what was making his van so bright but his dreadlocks got in the way.

"You didn't tell me my task?" I said.

"Oh, just pick Josie Miller to be your partner on next week's school trip."

"No way!" I said. "*No* way."

The Great Shaboosh went to take back my notebook.

"OK, OK," I said quickly. "I'll do it."

I didn't have a choice.

# Chapter 3

# Why Would You Sit Next to a Freak?

I waited till Mum went off to have her bath.

Then I went onto the computer and typed the magic link into the address bar. I was careful not to make any mistakes. Loud pop music started to pump out of the computer.

The screen turned yellow and shimmery. I yelled out with shock as a big cheerful face came up on my screen.

I was looking at a real live Magic Dad!

"Hi, I'm Andy!" he said with a grin. "Hope you like me! I'm a really happy fun guy. I love the open air life. I like riding trail bikes, snow boarding, white water rafting ..."

I started to smile to myself as Andy told me all the things he liked to do.

"I think life's a big adventure," he finished up. "I just need the right family to share it with me."

Andy's sun-tanned face froze into a still picture.

Gold writing came up under the picture, next to a flashing arrow.

"Download or cancel," I read aloud.

Why would I cancel? Andy was just what my mum was looking for! I clicked my mouse and waited to meet my cool new dad.

I waited all evening but nothing happened.

I was dropping off to sleep when it hit me.

"Duh! You have to do the task first, dummy!" I said to myself.

The hero only gets the princess after he kills the dragon! You need to do the task, then get the prize.

I sniggered into my pillow. *Freaky Josie was a bit like a dragon*, I thought. *Sitting next to her all day was going to be hard work.*

When I asked Josie if I could sit with her on the coach she snapped, "Why would you want to sit next to a freak?" Then she went back to her book.

But I'd promised the Great Shaboosh so I sat next to her anyway.

You should have seen the way the other kids looked at me. No one ever wanted to sit with Josie Miller. She was crazy. She had no style. Today she hadn't even brushed her hair.

I tried to talk to her but she just growled, "Stop bugging me!"

At the zoo our teachers took us to look at the penguins.

I stood next to Josie while the keeper threw fish to the penguins. "Check out the funky dinner jackets," I joked.

"I *said*, stop bugging me!" she told me.

"I'm just being friendly. Plus I hoped you'd help me out with the quiz. Your dad's a vet isn't he? You must know loads about animals."

"I'm not helping you! Do your own quiz," she scowled.

The keeper was telling us how dad penguins always take turns with mum penguins to look after the eggs.

It was raining now, big cold raindrops.

I heard Josie's teeth start to chatter.

"Put your coat on, dummy," I told her.

"My dad drove off with it by mistake," she shivered.

I gave her my jacket. "Put this on. I don't really feel the cold." Boys always say this kind of rubbish. I don't know why.

When the teachers took us into the reptile house I almost cheered! It's so hot and damp it's like a sauna in there!

At lunch-time I heard my mates snigger, like, "Ooh, Zack's got a girlfriend!"

"Where's your lunch?" I asked Josie.

"My dad drove off with my sandwiches too," she muttered.

"Have mine," I said with a sigh. "I'm not that hungry."

"What is it?" she asked as if she didn't trust me. "I've got allergies."

"Egg mayo."

She cheered up. "Oh, I can eat egg mayo."

My mum's sandwiches must have put her in a good mood because she suddenly said, "OK, I'll help you with your quiz, if you like."

Josie did know loads about animals. We got the most right answers out of everyone in the class!

My belly was rumbling by the time I got home.

*Hope Mum's made shepherd's pie,* I thought, as I let myself in.

"Zack, come and meet Andy!" Mum shouted.

I'd totally forgotten about Andy.

My Magic Dad was right here in my house!

# Chapter 4

## Wake Up, Dudes!

"Zack, my man!" Andy gave me a high five.

I was surprised to see Mum and Andy were both wearing tracksuits. I didn't know Mum had a tracksuit!

Mum told me she'd decided she had to stop feeling sorry for herself and get a life. She thought she'd feel better if she got fit, so she went down to join the gym.

"And she got me as her fitness instructor!" grinned Andy.

I wanted to laugh. Mum had NO idea she'd been set up!

I was about to die of hunger so I grabbed a packet of crisps and went to watch TV.

"Hey, dude! Put down those unhealthy carbs! Don't you know crisps are bad for you?" shouted Andy. "Let's go for a run while your mum makes the tea."

I looked at our big cosy sofa. It was raining outside.

"Oh, that'd be great!" I fibbed.

Two hours later I limped back in. I had mud all over me!

"I think you and Andy are going to be great friends," Mum whispered.

31

But now I'd met him in real life I thought Active Dad Andy was a bit *too* active.

I'd get home from school and he'd go, "Drop that TV remote, Zack, my man! Let's get some fresh air into those lungs!"

Then he'd drag us off roller blading or make us ride around for hours on trail bikes. Because he was a magic dad, Andy never got tired. He was like a playful puppy, always wanting to have fun.

One weekend he came to our house at six in the morning! He shouted up at our windows. "Wake up dudes! We're going camping!"

"It's winter! We'll freeze to death," Mum said.

"We won't! I've bought my Arctic sleeping bags!" Andy answered.

I said I'd go to please Mum.

But on the trip she didn't actually seem that happy ...

When we got back home she stopped answering Andy's calls. She let the machine pick up his jokey messages.

"Yo, dudes! Who's up for ice skating!!!" he'd say.

My mum said something rude, then had a sneezing fit. She'd caught a cold when we did the white water rafting.

"Andy's great fun – " Mum had to stop to blow her nose. "But he doesn't think how other people feel. A good dad is kind and thoughtful. He's sensitive. He understands that kids have feelings."

*That's not what she said before*, I thought. I gave a sigh, took out my notebook and got ready to write.

"What else?" I asked her.

It was time to go back to the Great Shaboosh.

# Chapter 5

## Life is Like a Sunset

The wizard didn't seem that surprised when I asked him to send Andy back.

He patted my shoulder. "Don't worry, we'll get the right dad this time. What else did she say? Sweet, kind ...?"

"He should really care about our feelings, run her a hot bath when she's upset, stuff like that."

"Oh, she's after a sensitive dad! That's where we were going wrong, Zack. We ordered the wrong dad!"

The Great Shaboosh wrote down a new link in my notebook. "Trust me, this one is perfect for her. Now, about your task ..."

"Want me to kill a dragon?" I asked.

He looked stern. "Did you ever hear of a hero who chose his own task? Magic has rules, Zack!"

"Sorry," I gulped. The Great Shaboosh could be scary sometimes.

"I want you to ask your mum to take you round to Josie's house. She's still got your jacket, remember."

"That's all?" I asked.

He gave me an odd smile. "Every journey starts with one small step."

"If you say so," I grinned. I had no idea what he was on about!

I almost ran back to the computer.

When I logged on to the Magic Dads website the screen turned deep rose pink. I could hear plinky guitar music.

A sweet-looking guy came up on my screen. He had floppy black hair and kind brown eyes. He was actually playing the guitar! Mum will *love* him, I thought.

"I am Raj," he said in a soft caring voice. "I'm a very peaceful person. When I get home from work I like to put on some music and cook a special meal for the people I love.

Life is like a beautiful sunset. It comes and goes so quickly. People should be kind and take care of each other."

"Jackpot!" I said aloud, and I clicked my mouse.

I went to tell Mum we needed to get my jacket back from Josie.

A muddy Jeep was parked outside Josie's house. It had these funky paw marks painted on the side so people could tell it belonged to a vet!

Josie's dad asked us in for a cup of tea.

Josie was sitting in a chair with three cats on her lap. She gave me a wave, and said, "I can't believe I forgot to give you back your coat!"

Her dad started to tell my mum a funny story about a woman who came into the vet's with a talking parrot. Every time the woman tried to tell Josie's dad what was wrong the parrot shouted, "She's lying!"

"My dad can really talk," Josie whispered.

"So can my mum," I hissed back and we both giggled.

One of their cats had just had kittens. Josie took me to see them. They were so new they didn't have their eyes open yet.

On the way home, Mum said, "That poor man doesn't have a clue about bringing up girls. Did you see Josie's clothes?"

I wasn't listening. I was picturing how happy Mum was going to be when she met Raj.

*******

When I got back from school the next day I was amazed to see Mum was wearing a floaty Indian dress and not her old jeans.

"I popped into the bookshop at lunch-time," she told me, "and the owner started chatting. He loves to cook so he's asked us over to his flat tonight. He's going to cook us a meal – isn't that sweet!"

The Great Shaboosh was so smooth! Mum totally believed she had just met Raj by luck!

Raj lived in a beautiful flat over the bookshop. There were candles flickering everywhere.

I was gutted when I saw the food. It was just vegetables!

Raj told me he didn't believe people should kill animals for food. He didn't believe you should hurt anything! "Everything in the Universe is alive, Zack, did you know that?"

41

"Ooh, is that your guitar?" I asked. I wanted him to shut up. "I bet Mum would love to hear you play!"

Raj asked me to help him make pancakes so we could get to know each other. I had room for tons of pancakes – we'd only had salad so far. But Raj said we had to decorate them first. He put out chopped cherries, nuts, marshmallows and maple syrup.

Raj drew a big heart on Mum's pancake with maple syrup, then decorated it with chopped nuts and cherries.

She went pink. "What a sweet thing to do," she murmered.

I thought it was a really wet thing to do but hey, I'm just a kid!

Raj started coming round to our house all the time. He always brought thoughtful little treats, cookies for me, a smelly scented candle for Mum.

"I want to make you guys happy," he kept telling my mum.

"We are, aren't we, Zack?" Mum said with a bright smile.

I started to hide upstairs in my room when he came over. But I could still smell those stinky candles.

Soon Raj was knocking on my door. "You seem upset, what's wrong?"

*I've got belly ache from too much salad, that's what's wrong!* I thought.

But I said, "No, I'm OK, really."

Raj looked worried. "Zack, you know you can tell me anything, don't you? I care about you. I need to know how you feel."

A sensitive dad sounds like a good thing, but sometimes a kid just wants to be left alone!

Then one day I was helping Raj make tea when Mum totally lost it! All he said was, "You look tired, my angel. Would you like me to run you a bubble bath?"

"I've got a name!" she yelled. "You don't have to call me your angel every time!"

Raj looked puzzled. "But you are my angel, I worship you!"

Mum stamped her foot. "I don't want to be worshipped! And you always ask what I want to do. You never tell me what you'd like to do."

"Yikes!" I yelled.

Blood was pouring out of my thumb. I'd cut myself with the knife.

"Sorry Raj," I said. "I think some of my blood went into your salad."

Raj fainted.

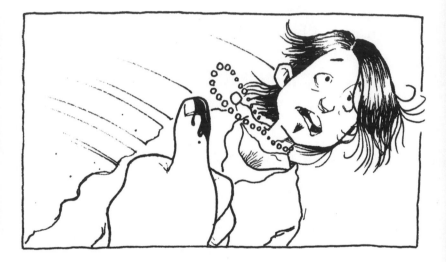

# Chapter 6

# The Last Magic Dad

The Great Shaboosh tut-tutted. "But Raj was so sweet and gentle! What didn't she like?"

"She says he was *too* gentle. Actually, she said he was a big wuss," I admitted.

The wizard looked tired. "Your mum isn't making this easy."

"Tell me about it! But it's OK, because this time I know just what we're looking for!"

I fished a DVD cover out of my jacket.

"Mum watched this movie with Aunt Sarah at the week-end and she really went for the hero."

"This guy?" said the Great Shaboosh in surprise. "He's old! And he looks really grumpy."

"Mum liked him because he doesn't talk about his feelings all the time like Raj, and he's really strong and silent." I grinned at the Great Shaboosh. "Plus he owns a massive country house so he has to be loaded!"

"Let's see if I've got this right," said the wizard. "Your mum thought she wanted a sensitive dad to run her bubble baths, but she really wanted an old-style strong silent dad with a big house?"

"Basically, yeah," I said.

It turned out the Magic Dads website had loads of old-style dads in stock.

"What's my task?" I asked. "Don't tell me I have to go and see Josie. She didn't come to school. She's ill."

"Ring her then, dummy," said the Great Shaboosh. "Say you'd like some help with your science project when she's feeling better."

"That's not a real task," I said. "Why don't you ever give me a real task? And don't say long journeys start with a small step!"

"Take it or leave it," he said softly. "By the way, three magic dads is your limit, so this is your last dad. Sorry, Zack."

But I knew we'd found Mum's ideal dad.

When I went on to the Magic Dads website, loud violin music almost blew my hair off. My screen became the colour of a dark and stormy sky.

A moody-looking man was sitting by a smoky log fire. "I don't like talking about myself so I'll keep it short. My name is Charles. I'm not an easy man to live with. I am also a – basket!"

He was shouting at his dog! I saw it slink past the webcam.

"Life is like a battle and a good father is like the captain of an army," Charles went on. I started to yawn. "He must be firm and fair and teach his children to obey his rules."

I stopped listening because Charles was really boring. If you had him for your dad, it would be like going right back to olden times.

But the guy in the movie was like Charles, and Mum said he was perfect. I wanted Mum to be happy, didn't I?

I took a deep breath and clicked DOWNLOAD.

Then I went to ring Josie.

"Hey, why weren't you at school?"

"Bad throat," she said. She sounded husky.

"My mum makes me honey drinks when I get a sore throat," I told her.

"I don't think Dad knows about honey drinks," Josie croaked sadly.

"Sorry," I said. "I didn't mean – "

"Oh, he's a great dad," Josie said. "He works so hard, that's all."

"I was going to ask if you could help with my science project," I said, "but if you're poorly ..."

"Come at the weekend," said Josie. "The kittens' eyes are open now."

"We might be busy at the weekend," I told her.

At the weekend Mum would be hooking up with boring Charles.

"Oh, right." Josie sounded unhappy.

I don't know why I felt so fed up suddenly.

Mum's dream was going to come true at last.

# Chapter 7

# Just Mum and Me Forever

On Friday afternoon when I got home Mum was in front of the mirror. She was wearing a tweed skirt, cardigan and pearls.

"Ooh, swanky!" I laughed.

Mum giggled. "I want to look smart for tomorrow. We're going to have lunch with a real lord! His name is Lord Crowfoot but he says I can call him Charles. I hope you'll like him."

"Do you like him?" I asked.

"I haven't met him," Mum admitted. "He bought one of my paintings from a gallery. He rang to say how much he liked it and we got on really well."

Next morning we drove for miles. It was windy and rainy. At last we saw a sign to Crowfoot Hall.

Charles came out with his dogs when he heard our car. He looked just as moody as he looked on the webcam.

"As you see, this house needs a woman's touch. Sorry," he said with a frown.

*It needs a good clean*, I thought, as we went inside.

Crowfoot Hall smelled of damp dogs and smoky fires. I could hear the wind howl outside.

Charles showed us into a big dark dining room then slammed out of the room without saying a word.

"I hope he's gone to get our lunch," Mum shivered.

After a while I heard a microwave beep and Charles came in with beans on toast! *And* the bread was mouldy. How mean was that!

We all ate in total silence and it wasn't a happy silence. Strong and silent is OK in movies but it's really stressful when you're eating. I started chatting because someone had to.

"These beans are *great*," I lied. "And the toast is really – different."

"Don't talk with your mouth full, boy! Basket!" he yelled suddenly.

One of his dogs was sniffing round my feet but Mum thought Charles was talking to me!

After we'd finished our food, Mum asked if we could sit by the fire. "Oh, you put my painting over the fireplace!" she cooed. "That one took me months, didn't it, Zack?"

That's when Charles blew his chances of ever being my dad.

"Of course, you won't have time to paint if you and Zack come to live with me at Crowfoot Hall."

Mum looked amazed. "But I love my work! And Zack's proud of me, aren't you, Zack?"

Charles shook his head. "A woman's duty is to care for her husband and child."

Mum put down her cup. "Thank you for our lovely beans," she said. "But Zack and I have to leave now."

She almost dragged me to the car.

"What century is that man living in?" she said as we went speeding down the drive.

The wind and rain seemed to follow us along the country lanes. Soon snowflakes were mixed up with the rain.

I was gutted. Charles wasn't Mum's Mr Right. He was Mr Totally Wrong. Mum had dumped him after exactly *one* hour! OK, I'd hated him too. But Charles was our last chance, our last Magic Dad. Now Mum would have to live alone with me forever.

********

Half way home our car broke down.

Mum's breakdown people said we'd have to wait an hour. After 20 minutes our teeth were chattering with cold.

Then a muddy Jeep loomed up out of the storm. My heart jumped as I saw the painted paw marks.

Josie's dad knocked on our window. "Need any help?"

# Chapter 8

# The Right Kind of Magic

"They were talking on the phone for hours again last night," Josie moaned. "They talk every night."

It was Sunday morning a few weeks later, and Josie and I had been talking on the phone for hours too.

There was a lot to talk about. Science projects. Names for the kittens. The surprise romance between our parents.

61

"I quite like your mum, Zack, do you quite like my dad?" Josie asked.

"Yeah, he's all right," I said.

Josie's dad didn't drag us off on mad adventures like Andy. He wasn't sweet and sensitive like Raj. He got really grumpy sometimes! But he wasn't moody and silent like Charles. Josie's dad could chat for England!

I liked him a lot. So did my mum!

I was looking out of my window while I was talking. The Great Shaboosh was outside doing something to his van.

I saw he had taken down his sign.

"Call you back later, Josie," I said.

I ran out of the house.

"So you just go round fixing up people's families, then you leave?" I shouted. "You don't even say good-bye?"

The wizard climbed up into the driving seat. "Is your family fixed?" he smiled. "That's excellent news, Zack!"

I remembered how Josie looked when my mum said she'd take her clothes shopping one week-end. She just grinned from ear to ear! And I remembered how good it felt when Josie's dad let me hold a sick puppy while he gave it an injection.

Was my family fixed? It was different, anyway.

"You planned this," I said. "You knew those Magic Dads wouldn't work out."

"That's because families need the right kind of magic if they're going to get along," the Great Shaboosh said with a smile.

"But how do you know when families have the right kind of magic?" I wanted to know.

I was trying to keep him talking. I wanted the Great Shaboosh to stay forever in case I needed him again.

"How do you know?" he asked softly. "Because it feels like coming home." Then he got back in the van and drove away.

I watched until the van was a tiny dot, then I walked back into the house.

Mum was in the kitchen in her scruffy old jeans. Josie and her dad were coming over for Sunday lunch.

The sun was shining through the window and the kitchen smelled of baked apples. And the Great Shaboosh was right. It felt like coming home.

Barrington Stoke would like to thank all its readers for commenting on the manuscript before publication and in particular:

Darren Bryan
Adam Buxton
Claire Carberry
Cynthia Clift
John Connor
Daniel Crowther
Patricia Davies
Courtney Edwards
Anne Gilchrist
Ryan Hanson
Ross Lacey

Gail MacLeod
Luke Ruane Maynard
Lee Moorhouse
Michael Obuya
Emily Parrish
Stephen Parsons
Elliott-John Shape
Akram Shiref
Nathan Yates
Charlotte Walker

## Become a Consultant!

Would you like to give us feedback on our titles before they are published? Contact us at the email address below – we'd love to hear from you!

info@barringtonstoke.co.uk
www.barringtonstoke.co.uk